THE WHITE HOUSE

WASHINGTON

Dear Hello Kitty,

We have heard many wonderful things about your very extraordinary piano playing, and commend your great achievement.

You and your accompanists are cordially invited to Washington, DC, to perform in our special upcoming gala celebration to honor the United States of America.

We look forward to seeing you.

Hello Kitty®

Hello USA!

illustrated by Higashi Glaser

HARRY N. ABRAMS, INC., PUBLISHERS

Hello
District of Columbia!
The Nation's Capital

The Washington Monument is the tallest monument in the capital at 550 feet high.

The Capitol Building is the home of the U.S. Congress.

reflecting pool

cherry blossoms

Washington, DC ★

American Beauty Rose
state flower

The White House, home to the President and his Cabinet, entertains world leaders, celebrities, and special citizens.

The Smithsonian Institution is the largest museum complex in the world.

Wood Thrush
state bird

Hello Kitty was invited to Washington, DC, to perform at a White House gala. The audience loved her piano performance and invited her to come back. She met many nice people there from all over the United States. They told her about their home states—and invited her to visit each one! Charmed by their warm hospitality, Hello Kitty and her friends decided to see America . . .

White Pine Tree
state tree

Hello
Maine!
The Pine Tree State

Mount Katahdin:
the first place to see dawn
in the U.S.

Maine has more
than 60 lighthouses.

Moose
state animal

Maine is the top
lobster producer
in the U.S.

Chickadee
state bird

Puffins live on Maine's
outlying islands.

White Pine Cone & Tassel
state flower

Maine has the largest black bear
population in the East.

Augusta

4

Hello
New Hampshire!
The Granite State

The Old Man of the Mountain remains a classic state symbol despite deterioration.

New Hampshire has over 50 covered bridges.

White Birch
state tree

Purple Lilac
state flower

White-tailed Deer
state animal

snowshoe hare

The alarm clock was invented in 1787.
Concord, NH

Purple Finch
state bird

Concord

Hello
Vermont!
The Green Mountain State

Monarch
state butterfly

Christmas trees

Vermont has the highest yield of wool in the Northeast.

Vermont has the most ski stations in New England.

Vermont has the greatest number of dairy cows in the country.

Vermont is famous for its maple syrup.

ice cream

XXX MAPLE

pure MAPLE SYRUP

Hermit Thrush
state bird

honey

honey

teddy bear

Red Clover
state flower

★ Montpelier

Hello
Massachussetts!
The Bay State

Basketball was invented in 1891.
Springfield, MA

Boston Marathon

Cape Cod

Volleyball was invented in 1895.
Holyoke, MA

Oldest U.S. Seaport
Gloucester, MA

The Boston Symphony is one of the nation's leading orchestras.

Plymouth Rock was the Pilgrims' landing spot.

The Wampanoag Indians joined the pilgrims for the first Thanksgiving feast, which lasted three days.

Black-Capped Chickadee
state bird

The first Thanksgiving was in 1621.

Ipswich Clams

Mayflower
state flower

Boston

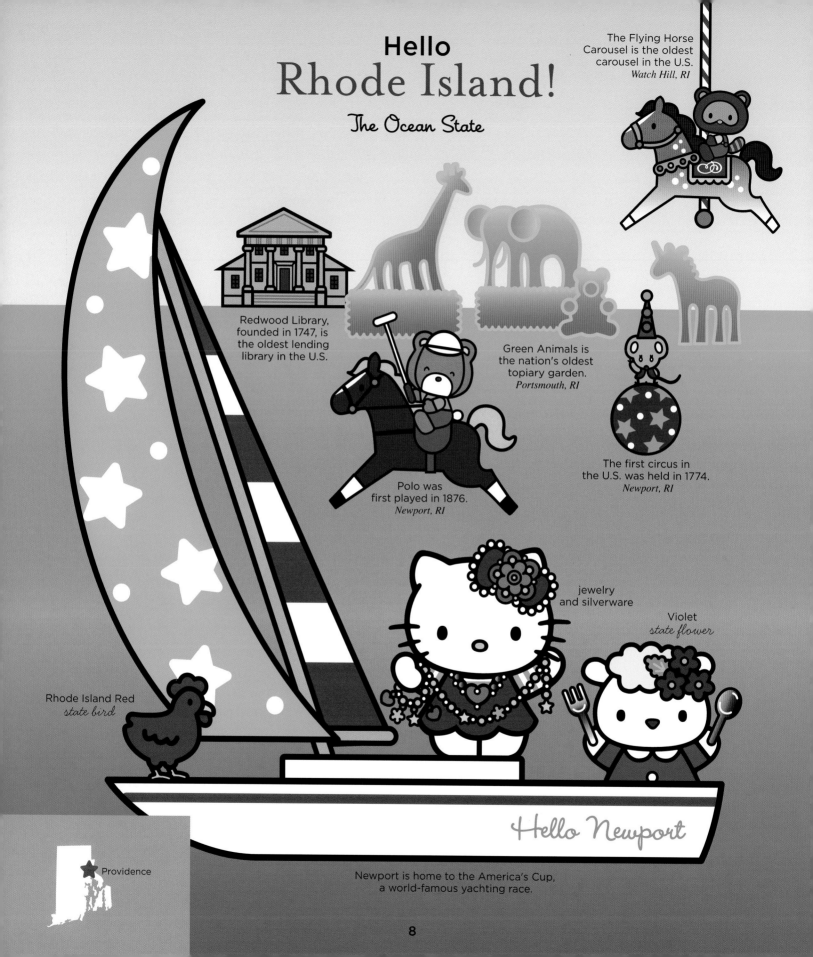

Hello
Rhode Island!
The Ocean State

The Flying Horse Carousel is the oldest carousel in the U.S.
Watch Hill, RI

Redwood Library, founded in 1747, is the oldest lending library in the U.S.

Green Animals is the nation's oldest topiary garden.
Portsmouth, RI

Polo was first played in 1876.
Newport, RI

The first circus in the U.S. was held in 1774.
Newport, RI

jewelry and silverware

Violet
state flower

Rhode Island Red
state bird

★ Providence

Hello Newport

Newport is home to the America's Cup, a world-famous yachting race.

8

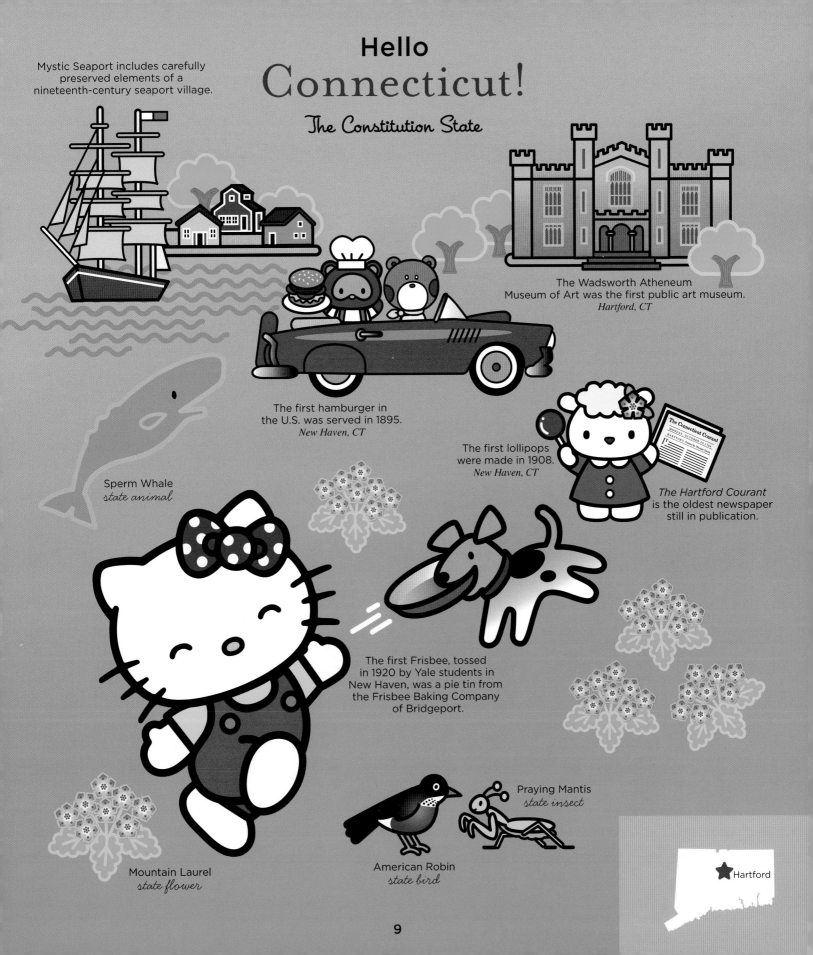

Hello
Connecticut!
The Constitution State

Mystic Seaport includes carefully preserved elements of a nineteenth-century seaport village.

The Wadsworth Atheneum Museum of Art was the first public art museum.
Hartford, CT

The first hamburger in the U.S. was served in 1895.
New Haven, CT

The first lollipops were made in 1908.
New Haven, CT

The Hartford Courant is the oldest newspaper still in publication.

Sperm Whale
state animal

The first Frisbee, tossed in 1920 by Yale students in New Haven, was a pie tin from the Frisbee Baking Company of Bridgeport.

Mountain Laurel
state flower

American Robin
state bird

Praying Mantis
state insect

★ Hartford

Hello
New York!

The Empire State

Niagara Falls lies on the border with Canada and measures 3,600 feet wide.

Broadway is home to more than 50 plays and musicals playing at any one time.

The Empire State Building is the tallest building in New York City.

TIMES SQUARE

New York City has more than 12,000 taxi cabs.

STOP

BROADWAY!

FASHION AVENUE

Bluebird
state bird

Hot dogs have been sold on pushcarts on New York City streets since the 1860s.

boutique

COUTURE

The Fashion District houses many famous designer showrooms.

Dedicated in 1886, the Statue of Liberty was a gift from France symbolizing freedom.

Apple
state fruit

New York cheesecake

Rose
state flower

Albany

Hello
New Jersey!
The Garden State

The Atlantic City Boardwalk is a popular amusement destination.

New Jersey is called "The Nation's Medicine Chest" because of its many pharmaceutical companies.

Legend states that salt water taffy got its name after the boardwalk flooded in 1883, and a shopkeeper so renamed his salt water-soaked candy.

beefsteak tomatoes

spinach

Atlantic City has played host to the Miss America Pageant since its beginning in 1921.

Miss America

lettuce

cranberries

blueberries

Purple Violet
state flower

Eastern Goldfinch
state bird

Trenton

11

Hello
Delaware!
The First State

American Holly
state tree

Delaware Bay has the most horseshoe crabs in the world.

The first log cabins were built in 1638 along the Delaware River Valley.

Enchanted Woods at Winterthur Garden

fresh

caramel corn

Tiger Swallowtail
state butterfly

In 1787, Delaware became the first of the original thirteen states to ratify the U.S. Constitution.

Lady Bug
state bug

Peach Blossom
state flower

Blue Hen
state bird

★ Dover

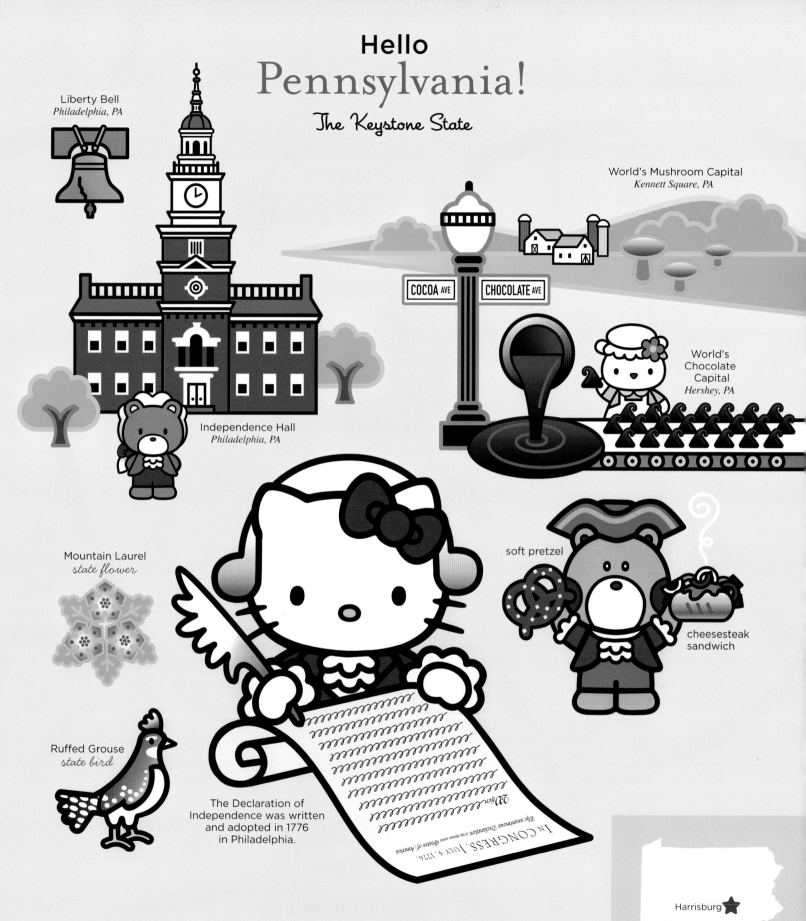

Hello
Pennsylvania!
The Keystone State

Liberty Bell
Philadelphia, PA

World's Mushroom Capital
Kennett Square, PA

COCOA AVE   CHOCOLATE AVE

World's
Chocolate
Capital
Hershey, PA

Independence Hall
Philadelphia, PA

Mountain Laurel
state flower

soft pretzel

cheesesteak
sandwich

Ruffed Grouse
state bird

The Declaration of
Independence was written
and adopted in 1776
in Philadelphia.

IN CONGRESS, JULY 4, 1776.
The unanimous Declaration of the thirteen united States of America

Harrisburg ★

13

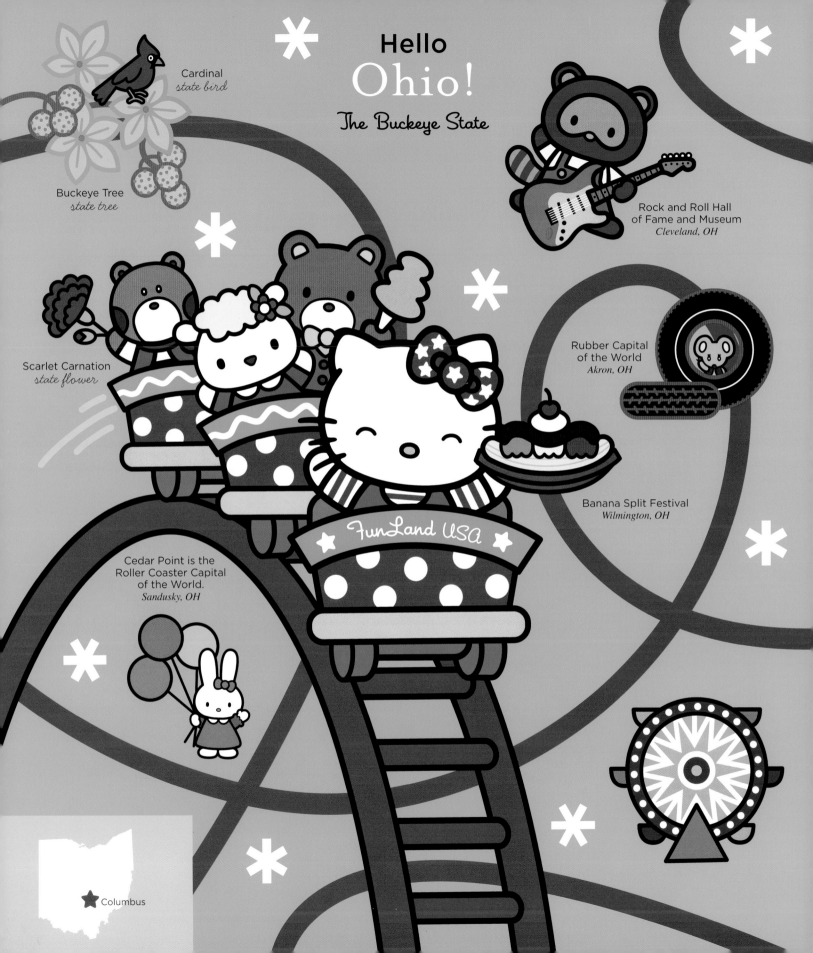

Hello
Ohio!
The Buckeye State

Cardinal
state bird

Buckeye Tree
state tree

Rock and Roll Hall
of Fame and Museum
Cleveland, OH

Scarlet Carnation
state flower

Rubber Capital
of the World
Akron, OH

Banana Split Festival
Wilmington, OH

Cedar Point is the
Roller Coaster Capital
of the World.
Sandusky, OH

FunLand USA

★ Columbus

Hello
West Virginia!
The Mountain State

Blackwater Falls are the largest falls in the state.

Appalachian Heritage Festival
Shepherdstown, WV

coal mining

glass blowing

Cardinal
state bird

white-water rafting

The New River is 350 million years old, the oldest river in the U.S.

Rhododendron
state flower

★ Charleston

Hello
Maryland!
The Old Line State

Baltimore National Aquarium has a collection of over 10,000 specimens and 500 species of marine life.

Assateague Island is home to wild horses.

Francis Scott Key wrote "The Star-Spangled Banner" in 1814.
Baltimore, MD

Baltimore Oriole
state bird

Black-Eyed Susan
state flower

blue crab

clams and oysters

Annapolis

16

Hello
Virginia!
The Old Dominion State

Chincoteague Island is known for its annual pony swim.

Mount Vernon was George Washington's home.
Alexandria, VA

Monticello was Thomas Jefferson's home.
Charlottesville, VA

Dogwood
state flower

White-tailed Deer

Virginia Peanut

Monticello's gardens were a botanic laboratory of plants from around the world.

Cardinal
state bird

Richmond

Hello
North Carolina!
The Tar Heel State

Dogwood
state flower

The Wright Brothers' first flight was in Kitty Hawk in 1903.

Cardinal
state bird

Furniture Capital of the World
High Point, NC

Jockey's Ridge State Park has the highest sand dunes in the eastern U.S.

North Carolina is one of the nation's top textile producers.

North Carolina grows more sweet potatoes than any other state.

The Cape Hatteras Lighthouse is the tallest in the nation.

Raleigh

Hello
Florida!
The Sunshine State

Popular theme
park destination
Orlando, FL

America's Launchpad
Cape Canaveral, FL

Brookgreen Gardens,
founded in 1931, was the
first public sculpture
garden in the U.S.

Sabal Palm
state tree

flamingo

Manatee
state mammal

Carolina Wren
state bird

South Carolina is the top peach
producer on the east coast.

Caro...
sta...

Orange Blossom
state flower

Miami

★ Tallahassee

Hello
Alabama!
Heart of Dixie

U.S. Space and Rocket Center
Huntsville, AL

The Birmingham Civil Rights Institute chronicles the civil rights movement.

Big Bass Fishing Capital
Lake Eufaula

Yellowhammer
state bird

Hello Kitty®

National Shrimp Festival
Gulf Shores, AL

Camellia
state flower

The boll weevil destroyed the state's cotton crop in 1915, but is celebrated for the crop diversity that resulted.

Cotton has played a key part in Alabama's history and is still the state's top crop.

★ Montgomery

Hello
Mississippi!
The Magnolia State

The Mississippi Sandhill Crane National Wildlife Refuge is the only place in the world that is home to this endangered bird.

Paddleboats, a major form of transportation on the Mississippi River in the 1900s, are still popular with tourists.

NORTH
61

SOUTH
49

Mississippi Mud Pie gets its name from its resemblance to cracked river mud.

The reknowned USA International Ballet Competition takes place in Jackson every four years.

Delta Blues Museum
Clarksdale, MS

Mockingbird
state bird

Catfish Capital of the World
Belzoni, MS

Magnolia
state flower

★ Jackson

Hello
Louisiana!
The Pelican State

The Birthplace of Jazz
New Orleans, LA

The French Quarter, famous for its Spanish-French architecture, is the oldest section in New Orleans.

Cajun Accordion
state musical instrument

Eastern Brown Pelican
state bird

The Mardi Gras festival is famous for its lively parade, colorful costume balls, and dancing in the streets.
New Orleans, LA

Gumbo Capital of the World
Bridge City, LA

Crawfish Capital of the World
South Louisiana

Magnolia
state flower

Beignets are a favorite New Orleans pastry.

Jambalaya Capital of the World
Gonzales, LA

Baton Rouge

24

Hello
Arkansas!
The Land of Opportunity

Crater of Diamonds State Park is the only public diamond field, where you can keep what you find!

Blanchard Springs Caverns is a "living cave" well known for its beauty.

Hot Springs National Park, nicknamed the American Spa, is known for its therapeutic springs.

Folk Music Capital of the World
Mountain View, AR

Duck Capital of the U.S.
White River, AR

Mockingbird
state bird

Apple Blossom
state flower

Home of the World's Largest Watermelons
Hope, AR

Arkansas is the top producer of rice in the U.S.

Little Rock ★

Hello
Tennessee!

The Volunteer State

The Grand Ole Opry is the world's longest-running live radio program.

Country Music Hall of Fame and Museum
Nashville, TN

BLUES
CLUB
Live Music

BB
Cafe

Beale Street is the birthplace of rock 'n' roll and the Home of the Blues.
Memphis, TN

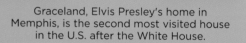

Graceland, Elvis Presley's home in Memphis, is the second most visited house in the U.S. after the White House.

The first miniature golf course was built in 1927.
Chattanooga, TN

Mockingbird
state bird

Iris
state flower

The Tennessee Aquarium was the world's first and largest freshwater aquarium.
Chattanooga, TN

★ Nashville

Hello
Kentucky!
The Bluegrass State

Red River Gorge is the most popular rock-climbing area in the east.

The National Corvette Museum showcases "America's Favorite Sports Car," and is next to the only plant where you can see them assembled.
Bowling Green, KY

International Bluegrass Music Museum
Owensboro, KY

The Kentucky Derby at Churchill Downs started in 1875, and continues to be one of the most famous horse races.
Louisville, KY

Horse Capital of the World
Lexington, KY

Cardinal
state bird

The Fort Knox Bullion Depository is one of the largest gold reserves in the nation.
Fort Knox, KY

24K
24K
24K

Goldenrod
state flower

Frankfort

Hello
Missouri!
The Show Me State

Honey Bee
state insect

Bluebird
state bird

The 630-foot-high Gateway Arch is the tallest U.S. monument and is known as the gateway to the West.

Lewis and Clark began their expedition on the Missouri River.

Hawthorn
state flower

Fiddle
state instrument

Old Courthouse
St. Louis, MO

Largest Beer Brewery
St. Louis, MO

Dogwood
state tree

Jefferson City

Mule
state animal

28

Hello
Iowa!
The Hawkeye State

Iowa leads the nation in soybean production.

Cattle is an integral part of Iowa's economy.

Eastern Goldfinch
state bird

Iowa is the nation's top corn producer.

Iowa is the top egg producer in the U.S.

There are over 15 million hogs in Iowa.

Wild Rose
state flower

★ Des Moines

Hello Illinois!

The Prairie State

Cardinal
state bird

The Lincoln Home National Historic Site was Abraham Lincoln's residence until he became President.
Springfield, IL

Illinois is the second largest corn producer in the U.S., after Iowa.

Jay Pritzker Pavilion

Millenium Park is Chicago's state-of-the-art cultural and entertainment center.

Cloud Gate
by Anish Kapoor

cookies & crackers

Pumpkin
Capital of the World
Morton, IL

The Crown Fountain

candy & gum

Chicago-style pizza

Native Violet
state flower

The Sears Tower is North America's largest building.
Chicago, IL

Springfield

Hello
Indiana!
The Hoosier State

Mid-America Windmill Museum
Kendallville, IN

The nation's top producer of steel, Indiana manufactured several makes of now-classic cars in the early twentieth century.

The Circus Capital of the World
Peru, IN

The Lincoln Museum has largest private collection of Lincoln memorabilia.
Fort Wayne, IN

The Indianapolis 500 is the oldest and most famous auto race in the world.

Indiana is one of the top popcorn producers in the nation.

Cardinal
state bird

Peony
state flower

★ Indianapolis

Hello
Michigan!
The Wolverine State

Birthplace of Motown
Detroit, MI

Michigan, which borders four of the five Great Lakes, has more recreational boats than any other state.

The Detroit Zoo was the first cageless zoo in the U.S.

The Cereal Capital of the World
Battle Creek, MI

Apple Blossom
state flower

American Robin
state bird

Detroit, nicknamed Motor City, is home to the top three car makers in the U.S.

Tulip Time is one of the largest floral festivals in the U.S.
Holland, MI

★Lansing

Hello
Wisconsin!
The Badger State

The first snowmobile was invented by Wisconsin native Carl Eliason in 1924.

The American Birkebeiner, also called "The Birkie," is the largest cross-country ski race in North America.

American Robin
state bird

Jump Rope Capital of the World
Bloomer, WI

Wisconsin is one of the largest dairy and cheese producers in the country.

MILK

Swiss Cheese Capital of the United States
Monroe, WI

Wood Violet
state flower

Birthplace of the Ice Cream Sundae
Two Rivers, WI

★ Madison

Hello
Minnesota!

The North Star State

Water skis were invented by Ralph Samuelson in 1922.
Lake City, MN

MALL OF AMERICA

Mall of America is the largest retail and entertainment complex in the country.
Bloomington, MN

Molecule sculpture

Spoonbridge & Cherry sculpture

Amaryllis sculpture

The Minneapolis Sculpture Garden is the largest urban sculpture garden in the U.S.

boutique

gourmet

The first automatic pop-up toaster was invented by Charles Strite in 1919.
Stillwater, MN

Minnesota is the nation's top producer of sugar beets.

Common Loon
state bird

Pink & White Lady's Slipper
state flower

The Mayo Clinic is one of the most famous and respected hospitals in the world.
Rochester, MN

★ St. Paul

Hello
North Dakota!
The Peace Garden State

The Enchanted Highway features the world's largest metal sculptures.
Regent, ND

The International Peace Garden on the U.S.-Canadian border is a symbol of peace and friendship.

The National Buffalo Museum features the world's largest buffalo sculpture.
Jamestown, ND

Wild Prairie Rose
state flower

Turtle Racing Championship
Turtle Lake, ND

Western Meadowlark
state bird

The United Tribes International Powwow is one of the nation's largest Native American celebrations.
Bismarck, ND

Norsk Hostfest is the biggest Scandinavian Festival on the continent.
Minot, ND

North Dakota is the top sunflower producer in the U.S.

★ Bismarck

Hello
South Dakota!

The Coyote State

The Crazy Horse Memorial is the world's largest sculpture.

mountain goat

bald eagle

Black Hills

Custer State Park is home to over 1,500 free-roaming bison.

Ring-necked Pheasant
state bird

Mount Rushmore features carvings of Presidents Washington, Jefferson, Lincoln, and Theodore Roosevelt.
Keystone, SD

coyote

Pasque Flower
state flower

★ Pierre

Hello
Nebraska!
The Cornhusker State

corn

Nebraska is the nation's top beef producer.

Nebraska has 11,000 miles of flowing streams.

wild plums and choke cherries

prairie dog

The first Arbor Day was celebrated in 1872.
Nebraska City, NB

mink

Western Meadowlark
state bird

bobcat

Goldenrod
state flower

Lincoln ★

37

Hello
Kansas!
The Sunflower State

Western Meadowlark
state bird

The midpoint of the contiguous forty-eight states is near Lebanon, Kansas.

EAST ← WEST →

Amelia Earhart, a native of Atchison, in 1932 became the first woman to fly solo across the Atlantic Ocean.

Kansas is one of the leading aviation aircraft producers.

Native Sunflower
state flower

Kansas is the second largest producer of beef cattle after Texas.

The Oz Museum houses one of the largest collections of memorabilia from the movie *The Wizard of Oz.*
Wamego, KS

Topeka ⭐

"The Breadbasket of the Nation," Kansas is the nation's leading winter wheat producer.

Hello
Oklahoma!
The Sooner State

Salt Plains National Wildlife Refuge is a globally important bird area.

Route 66, nicknamed "The Mainstreet of America," was the brainchild of Tulsa native Cyrus Avery.

Diner

MOTEL

ROUTE 66

GAS

Spiro Mounds is a renowned prehistoric Indian site.
Spiro, OK

Oklahoma has several museums and events devoted to preserving its very important Native American heritage.

Scissor-tailed Flycatcher
state bird

The National Cowboy Hall of Fame and Western Heritage Museum preserves the spirit of the frontier.
Oklahoma City, OK

The International Gymnastics Hall of Fame
Oklahoma City, OK

Mistletoe
state flower

Oklahoma City

Hello
Texas
The Lone Star State

NASA/Johnson Space Center is headquarters for America's manned space program.
Houston, TX

Texas is the largest natural gas producer and second-largest oil producer in the U.S.

The Alamo is considered a "Shrine of Texas Liberty."

Texas is the largest cattle producer in the U.S.

Chili
state dish

Mockingbird
state bird

Texas is the top cotton producer in the country.

Armadillo
state mammal

Bluebonnet
state flower

Austin

Hello
New Mexico
Land of Enchantment

The "Birthplace of the Race to Space"
White Sands, NM

UFO museums
Roswell, NM

Chile Capital of the World
Hatch, NM

The Ceremonial Capital of Native America
Gallup, NM

Albequerque International Balloon Fiesta is the largest hot air balloon festival in the world.

ROUTE 66

Roadrunner
state bird

Yucca
state flower

The Whole Enchilada Festival celebrates New Mexico's traditions, culture, and food.
Las Cruces, NM

★ Santa Fe

Hello
Colorado!
The Centennial State

Colorado is a major wintering area for bald eagles.

The Colorado Rockies have fifty-one peaks over 14,000 feet high, called "fourteeners" by climbers.

Mesa Verde, or "green table," National Park, is a cliff-dwelling preserve, originally inhabited from 600 CE to 1300 CE.

The Nation's Largest Ski Resort
Vail, CO

Bighorn Sheep
state mammal

Colorado has the largest population of bighorn sheep in the U.S.

Rocky Mountain Columbine
state flower

Lark Bunting
state bird

Colorado is the White Water Capital of the World.

★ Denver

Hello Wyoming!
The Cowboy State

Grand Teton National Park

Devils Tower was America's first national monument.

Old Faithful, in Yellowstone National Park, is the world's most famous geyser.

National Elk Refuge
Jackson Hole, WY

Rodeo
state sport

Many black bears and grizzlies live in and around Yellowstone and Grand Teton Parks.

Bison
state mammal

Indian Paintbrush
state flower

Meadowlark
state bird

Cheyenne

Hello Montana!

The Treasure State

Montana has the most golden eagles in the country.

Glacier National Park is one of the largest intact ecosystems in the U.S.

Trumpeter Swans

Miles City is rich with cowboy culture and events, such as the Bucking Horse Sale.

Egg Mountain is famous for its concentration of dinosaur fossils.

Western Meadowlark
state bird

Montana, with 700 miles of trails, and over a million acres of forests, alpine meadows, and lakes, is an outdoor lover's paradise.

The first luge run in the U.S. was built in Lolo Hot Springs in 1965.

Snow Goose

Bitteroot
state flower

★ Helena

Hello
Idaho!
The Gem State

The Snake River Canyon has America's largest concentration of birds of prey.

Hells Canyon is the deepest river gorge in the U.S.

Sun Valley, America's first ski resort, also had the world's first alpine chairlift in 1936.

Shoshone Falls is nicknamed "Niagara of the West."

Craters of the Moon National Monument is the largest basaltic lava field in the United States.

Mountain Bluebird
state bird

Idaho is the top producer of potatoes in the U.S.

Syringa
state flower

★ Boise

Hello
Utah!
The Beehive State

Rainbow Bridge, a national monument, is a sacred Navajo symbol of desert life, and one of the seven natural wonders of the world.

Thanksgiving Point houses the world's largest dinosaur museum.
Lehi, UT

The Great Salt Lake is four times more salty than the ocean.

Monument Valley Tribal Park

Many ancient Indian petroglyphs can be found throughout the state.

Moab Slickrock Bike Trail is one of the nation's most famous bike trails.

California Seagull
state bird

Sego Lily
state flower

★ Salt Lake City

46

Hello
Arizona!

The Grand Canyon State

The Grand Canyon is over two million years old and the most visited national park in the U.S.

Monument Valley Tribal Park is part of the Navajo Reservation, the largest in the U.S.

The Painted Desert's colors are created by its mineral, plant, and animal fossils from the Triassic Era.

Cactus Wren
state bird

cantaloupe

The Bola Tie
state neckwear

Saguaro Cactus Blossom
state flower

Arizona is the nation's largest producer of turquoise.

★ Phoenix

Hello
Nevada
The Silver State

WELCOME

CABARET

Hotel

CASINO

Hoover Dam

Las Vegas is popular for its 24-hour gambling and entertainment, and for its over-the-top hotels.

The National Bowling Stadium is also dubbed "The Taj Mahal of Tenpins." *Reno, NV*

Mountain Bluebird
state bird

Nevada is the nation's largest producer of both silver and gold.

24K 24K 24K

Sagebrush
state flower

★ Carson City

Hello
California

The Golden State

The Golden Gate Bridge, at 9,266 feet long, is one of the world's largest suspension bridges.

Yosemite Falls is the highest waterfall in North America. *Yosemite National Park.*

Redwood National Park is home to the world's tallest tree, a 367-foot-high Sequoia.

HOLLYWOOD

BAKERY

CAPITOL RECORDS

Hollywood is the hub of the movie and television industries.

Venice Beach's 22-mile bike path is famous for in-line skating.

California Valley Quail
state bird

FREEWAY

INTERSTATE
405

California has more automobiles and miles of highway than any other state.

groceries

MILK

California is the top avocado, artichoke, asparagus, peach, and milk producer in the U.S.

Golden Poppy
state flower

Death Valley has the highest recorded temperature, 165 degrees Farenheit, and gets less than two inches of rain per year.

★ Sacramento

Hello
Oregon!
The Beaver State

Western Meadowlark
state bird

Oregon, half-covered in forest, is the leading lumber state.

Crater Lake is the deepest lake in the U.S.

Oregon is one of the top producers of Christmas trees.

Beaver
state animal

Oregon is the top hazelnut producer in the U.S.

Chinook Salmon are found all along the coast of Oregon.

★ Salem

Oregon Grape
state flower

Hello
Washington!
The Evergreen State

After a century of dormancy, the Mount St. Helens volcano errupted in 1980.

The Peace Arch, built in 1921, was the first monument dedicated to world peace.

The Space Needle in Seattle was built for the 1962 World's Fair.

Willow Goldfinch
state bird

Washington is the country's top sweet cherry producer.

Washington is the largest producer of apples in the U.S.

Washington is the nation's leading pear producer.

Octopi found in the Puget Sound are the world's largest.

Western Rhododendron
state flower

★ Olympia

Hello
Alaska!
North to the Future

Aurora Borealis, or the Northern Lights, is most visible in Alaska.

Polar bears frequent the ice and tundra of the extreme north and west of Alaska.

Mt. McKinley is the higest point in North America.

The Tongass National Forest is the largest forest in the U.S.

caribou

Willow Ptarmigan
state bird

puffin

The annual Iditarod Dog Sled Race from Anchorage to Nome, AK, commemorates the heroic 1925 delivery of life-saving medicine.

Walrus Islands are world famous for their large walrus population.

Forget-Me-Not
state flower

Abundant salmon, trout, and halibut are why Alaska has the largest fishing industry in the U.S.

Kodiak, the world's largest brown bears, are exclusive to Alaska's Kodiak Island.

Juneau

Hello
Hawaii!
The Aloha State

Hawaii has about fifteen species of wild dolphins.

Kilauea Volcano, in the Hawaii Volcanoes National Park, is the world's most active volcano.

Hula dancing is a traditional Polynesian dance of worship.

Hawaii is the only coffee bean-growing state in the nation.

Hawaii is the leading sugar cane producer in the U.S.

Hawaii is the top pineapple producer in the U.S.

About forty species of sharks live around the Hawaiian islands.

Hawaii produces 90 percent of the world's macadamia nuts.

Hawaii's hundreds of miles of prime beaches attract vacationers worldwide.

Hawaiian Goose
state bird

Hawaii is internationally famous for its surfing.

Hibiscus
state flower

Green "Honu" Turtle

Honolulu

53

Hello Kitty and her friends enjoyed their trip around the United States.

They met nice people everywhere and did all kinds of fun activities. But there is so much more to see! Hello Kitty invites you to explore America yourself, to discover more wonderful surprises.

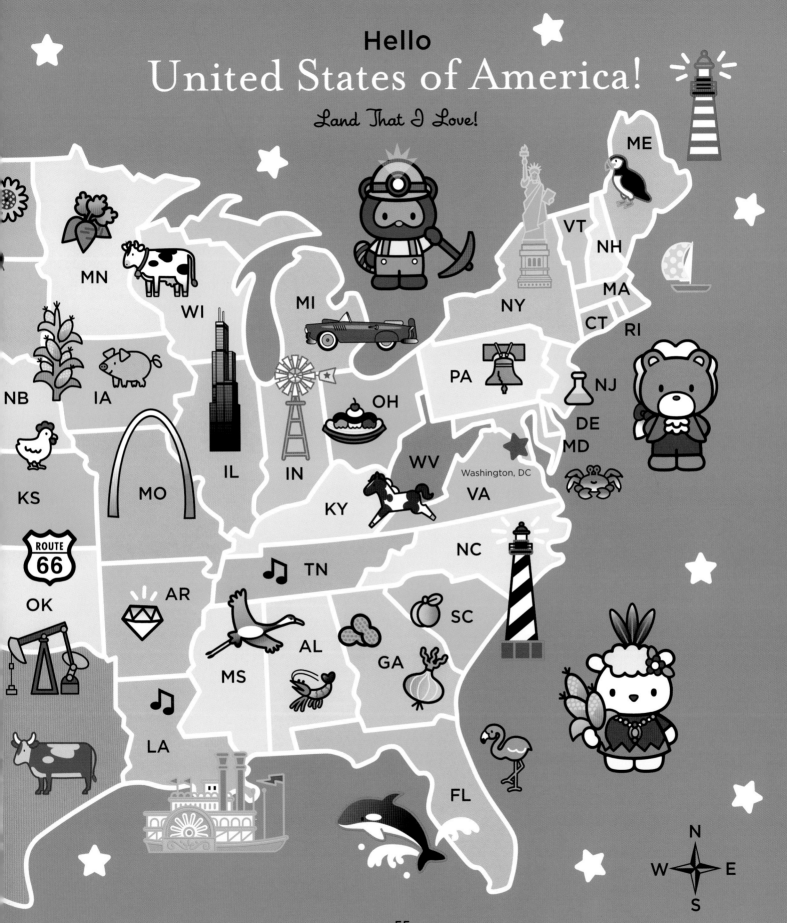

Hello
United States of America!
Land That I Love!

MN · WI · MI · ME · VT · NH · NY · MA · CT · RI · PA · NJ · DE · MD · NB · IA · OH · WV · Washington, DC · VA · IL · IN · KY · NC · KS · MO · TN · SC · OK · AR · AL · GA · MS · LA · FL

ROUTE 66

N · W · E · S

Hello Kitty visited the states one by one, beginning in the northeast and then driving south then west. For easy page reference, here are the states in alphabetical order:

Library of Congress Cataloging-in-Publication Data has been applied for.
ISBN 0-8109-5772-8

Hello Kitty® characters, names, and all related indicia are trademarks of Sanrio Co., Ltd.
Used under license. Copyright ©1976, 2005 Sanrio Co., Ltd.

Text and original art copyright ©2005 Harry N. Abrams, Inc.
Design and illustration by Higashi Glaser Design

Printed and bound in China
10 9 8 7 6 5 4 3 2 1

ABRAMS HARRY N. ABRAMS, INC.
100 FIFTH AVENUE
NEW YORK, NY 10011
www.abramsbooks.com

Abrams is a subsidiary of
LA MARTINIÈRE
GROUPE